Welcome to
Charlie!

May the vast
narratives and imagery
of life
never frighten you!

♡ Aunt Sophie

LIFE DOESN'T FRIGHTEN ME

Poem by

MAYA ANGELOU

Paintings by

JEAN-MICHEL BASQUIAT

Edited by
SARA JANE BOYERS

LIFE DOESN'T FRIGHTEN ME

Twenty-fifth Anniversary Edition

ABRAMS BOOKS FOR YOUNG READERS • NEW YORK

The Library of Congress has cataloged the original 1993 hardcover edition as follows:
Angelou, Maya
Life doesn't frighten me / by Maya Angelou; paintings by Jean-Michel Basquiat;
edited by Sara Jane Boyers.
p. cm
Includes bibliographical references.
Summary: Presents Maya Angelou's poem illustrated by paintings and drawings
of Jean-Michel Basquiat. Features biographies of both author and artist.
ISBN 978-1-55670-288-4
1.Fear—Juvenile poetry. 2. Children's poetry, American. [1. Fear—poetry. 2. American poetry.
3. Angelou, Maya. 4. Authors, American. 5. Afro-Americans—Biography.
6. Basquiat, Jean Michel. 7. Artists.] I. Basquiat, Jean-Michel, ill. II. Boyers, Sara Jane.
III. Title.
PS3551.N464L54   1993
811'.54-dc20   92-40409
ISBN for this 2017 hardcover edition: 978-1-4197-2748-1

Book design by Tree Abraham
Original book design by Paul Zakris

Published in 2017 by Abrams Books for Young Readers, an imprint of ABRAMS.

Printed and bound in China
10 9 8 7 6 5 4 3 2 1

Abrams Books for Young Readers are available at special discounts when purchased
in quantity for premiums and promotions as well as fundraising or educational use.
Special editions can also be created to specification.
For details, contact specialsales@abramsbooks.com or the address below.

ABRAMS The Art of Books
195 Broadway, New York, NY 10007
abramsbooks.com

For Morgan and Lily Kate
—S. J. B.

Shadows on the wall
Noises down the hall

LIFE

DOESN't

FRIGHTEN

ME

AT ALL

Bad dogs barking loud

Big ghosts in a cloud

LIFE DOESN'T FRIGHTEN ME AT ALL.

Mean old Mother Goose

Lions on the loose

THEY DON'T FRIGHTEN ME AT ALL

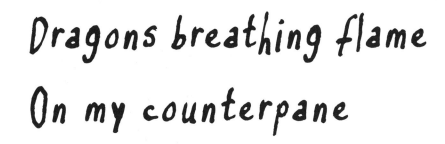

Dragons breathing flame
On my counterpane

THAT DOESN'T FRIGHTEN ME AT ALL,

I go boo
Make them shoo
I make fun
Way they run
I won't cry
So they fly
I just smile
They go wild

LIFE DOESN'T
FRIGHTEN ME
AT ALL.

Tough guys in a fight
All alone at night
LIFE DOESN'T
FRIGHTEN ME
AT ALL.

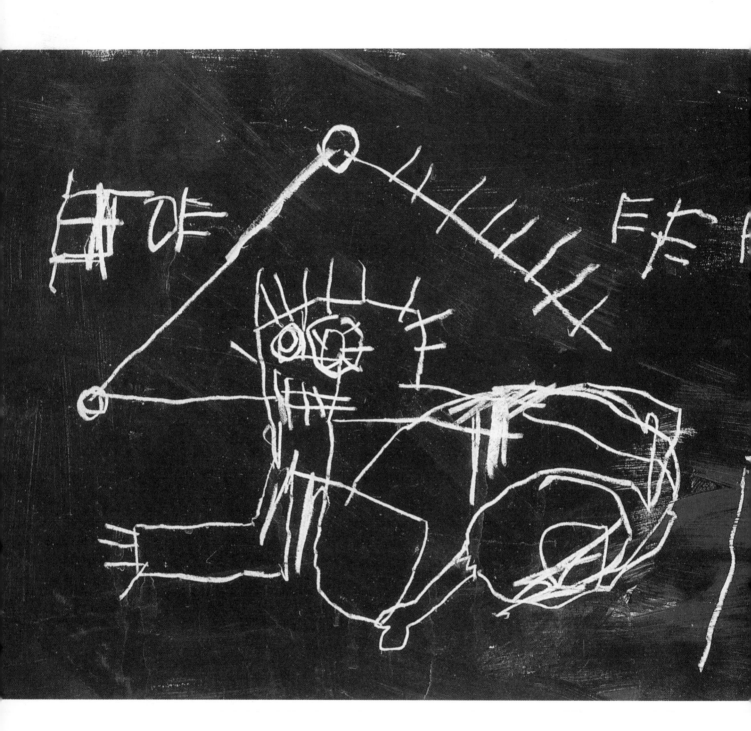

Panthers in the park

Strangers in the dark
NO, THEY DON'T FRIGHTEN ME AT ALL.

That new classroom where
Boys all pull my hair
(Kissy little girls
With their hair in curls)

THEY DON'T FRIGHTEN ME AT ALL.

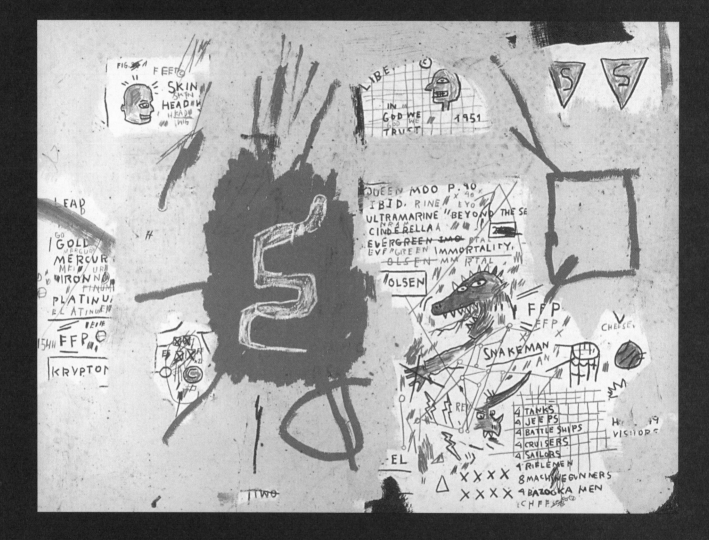

Don't show me the frogs and snakes
And listen for my scream,
If I'm afraid at all
It's only in my dreams.

I've got a magic charm
That I keep up my sleeve,

I can walk the ocean floor
And never have to breathe.

LIFE DOESN'T FRIGHTEN ME AT ALL

Not at all

Not at all.

LIFE DOESN'T FRIGHTEN ME AT ALL.

MAYA

ANGELOU

Dr. Maya Angelou (1928–2014) was a poet, writer, performer, civil rights advocate, and professor whose words and deeds have made a lasting impression on American society.

Dr. Maya Angelou experienced a challenging early childhood, faced with her parents' separation and the ever-present cloud of racism. Yet, fortified by the nurturing support of her grandmother, mother, and brother, Angelou thrived.

For much of their early childhood years, Angelou and her older brother lived with their paternal grandmother in Stamps, Arkansas, where race relations had little improved since the Civil War. Against this turbulent backdrop, the children were raised in a proud, industrious family, led by their grandmother and steeped in the world of literature:

Paul Laurence Dunbar, Langston Hughes, W. E. B. Du Bois, the Brontës, Mark Twain, and Shakespeare.

Following a traumatic assault at age seven, Angelou stopped speaking for five years. Later, she said of that time, "I stopped talking, but I could hear … when I decided to speak again, I had a lot to say."

Thankfully, Angelou never chose silence over action again. After bearing a son at age sixteen, Angelou worked tirelessly to support her family. She worked as a cook, waitress, actress, singer, and dancer, wisely choosing musical genres where she would be most noticed—such as calypso, then a popular musical trend.

From 1959 to 1960, Dr. Angelou served as the Northern Coordinator of Dr. Martin Luther King Jr.'s Southern Christian Leadership Conference. As activism spread worldwide, she traveled to Europe, the Middle East, and Africa where, in Ghana, she became the first female editor of an English-language newsweekly and later a professor at the University of Ghana. Returning to the United States in the late 1960s, she found the country in the midst of increasingly contrasting movements: the Black Nationalism promoted by Malcolm X and the nonviolent integration of Dr. King. A friend to both men, Dr. Angelou often acted as the philosophical bridge between them.

Dr. Angelou was named the first Reynolds Professor of American Studies at Wake Forest University in Winston-Salem, North Carolina, a lifetime position she held for more than thirty years. Until her death in 2014, she wrote, lectured, protested, and performed passionately worldwide, advocating always for the rights of all to be exercised with perseverance and civility. Among her many accolades and accomplishments are Dr. Angelou's powerful poem, "On the Pulse of Morning," commissioned by President Bill Clinton for his inauguration, only the second poem ever so commissioned by a U.S. president; and the Presidential Medal of Freedom, awarded to Dr. Angelou in 2011 by President Barack Obama.

With eloquence and immediacy, Maya Angelou has shared her own life story in a series of strong autobiographies, beginning with the acclaimed *I Know Why the Caged Bird Sings.* In all her work, she shares her passion and exuberance, her defeats and triumphs, so that all may feel her vitality, humor, and faith. Her advice, not only to writers but also to everyone: to read everything possible, be it African American, European, Latino, or other literature—but especially Shakespeare.

Life, she feels, is one's sole possession, and it certainly never frightened Maya Angelou.

Selected Bibliography of Maya Angelou's Books

The Complete Collected Poems of Maya Angelou. New York: Random House, 1994.

I Know Why the Caged Bird Sings. New York: Random House, 1969.

Letter to My Daughter. New York: Random House Trade Paperbacks, 2009.

Mom & Me & Mom (1st ed.). New York: Random House, 2013.

On the Pulse of Morning. New York: Random House, 1993.

Selected Media

Maya Angelou: And Still I Rise. Documentary by Bob Hercules and Rita Coburn Whack for American Masters/PBS, 2016.

JEAN MICHEL BASQUIAT

Jean-Michel Basquiat (1960–1988) grew up in Brooklyn, New York. His middle-class Haitian father and Puerto Rican mother introduced him to visual art, music, and theater as a young child.

From the age of four, Basquiat drew incessantly, forming his lifelong habit of filling notebooks with notes, lists, titles, poetry, short stories, cartoons, drawings, and music references of all sorts—the notebooks often becoming pieces of the artist's artwork themselves.

As a teenager, Basquiat left home to live in downtown Manhattan, sometimes on the streets and sometimes with friends, selling hand-painted postcards and T-shirts to support himself and his artwork. With a friend, he created the tag "SAMO©," drawing and lettering on building walls throughout lower Manhattan and Brooklyn.

Later, as Basquiat left SAMO© behind, his art continued to reflect influences of the city, as well as the African, French, and Latino-Caribbean traditions of his parents' homelands. He reintroduced body imagery to art, featuring black bodies that had rarely been shown in modern American art.

Anything and everything Basquiat encountered found its way into his art: words and images from television, film, politics, and sports; his collections of books—especially *Gray's Anatomy*, a gift from his mother as he convalesced from an early childhood accident; films, old photographs, rare toys; the music of jazz, rock, and hip-hop that he heard and played; and even photocopies of his own and other artists' works. He frequently repeated images, such as teeth, crowns, and arrows, and they soon became identified with his art.

The artist's powerful paintings and drawings, often imbued with poetic meaning, expressed a range of emotions, from humor to anger. Using unexpected media and materials, Basquiat became known for weaving together the rhythms and textures of the city, the techniques and traditions of the fine arts, and the cultures that so often inspired him. One of the first black artists to break through the racial barriers of the fine art world, Basquiat quickly rose to fame.

With his first one-person exhibition in 1982, the art world discovered Basquiat, drawing connections to many of the great artists of the first half of the twentieth century: Jean Dubuffet, Jasper Johns, Willem de Kooning, and especially Pablo Picasso.

Yet, as his career grew, Basquiat's complicated relationship with this fast fame did not always serve him well. And while he was proud of his growing renown and rejoiced with his family and friends, the pressures on him increased. After an accidental drug overdose, the artist tragically died at the young age of twenty-seven.

Today, Jean-Michel Basquiat is considered one of the greatest artists of the late twentieth century and is one of the most exhibited ever. The iconic symbolism of his work continues to resonate with the issues of contemporary society and inspires many in the worlds of art, culture, and fashion. Expressively bringing to the forefront complicated and multidimensional subjects, Basquiat's art depicts the world as he perceived it: diverse, funny, raucous, poetic, and potentially scary—but always real.

Selected Museum Collections of the Work of Jean-Michel Basquiat

Barcelona Museum of Contemporary Art, Barcelona

The Broad, Los Angeles

Centre Pompidou, Paris

Daros Collection, Zurich

Guggenheim Museum Bilbao, Spain

Menil Collection, Houston

Museum of Contemporary Art, Los Angeles

Museum of Fine Arts, Montreal

Museum of Modern Art, San Francisco

Rubell Family Collection, Miami

Whitney Museum of American Art, New York City

Selected Media

The Art of Jean-Michel Basquiat, by Fred Hoffman. Paris: Galerie Enrico Navarra, 2017.

Downtown 81. Feature film directed by Edo Bertoglio, written by Glenn O'Brien, produced by O'Brien and Maripol. Zeitgeist, 1981 (currently distributed by Music Box Films).

Jean-Michel Basquiat: The Radiant Child. Documentary film directed by Tamra Davis. Arthouse Films/Curiously Bright Entertainment/LM Media, 2010.

Afterword

Life Doesn't Frighten Me is about life experience. It is about perseverance and pride, finding oneself within one's own life story, the good and the bad, and using everything that influences or affects us—our families, our culture, our everyday world—to constantly reinvent and support ourselves. It is a reflection on the artwork of two legendary black artists from very different worlds with vastly different experiences and economic and aesthetic backgrounds. Their unique artistic works, often originally marginalized by race, are strong expressions of overcoming obstacles just to be seen and heard. Pairing their work here created a new story for them—a new story for each of us—and it invites us all to pen our own stories, on our own terms.

Because it's about us. Whoever we are, however we are categorized, whatever we look like, wherever we come from, and whatever language(s) we speak, *Life Doesn't Frighten Me* addresses the universals of our lives and how we can use everything we see, feel, hear, touch, and encounter on all of our paths. In many ways, these are the "magic charms" that give us the hope, understanding, and resolve to be us, together.

In *Life Doesn't Frighten Me*, Jean-Michel Basquiat and Maya Angelou, through their own individual work, converse with each other in new and vital ways. You can also join in the conversation, for we each bring to the table our own history, talents, and perspectives. This is exactly what art and poetry should be: a bit of the creator, and a lot of us.

Let's keep talking!
Sara Jane Boyers

Sara Jane Boyers

A California-based writer/editor, internationally exhibiting fine art photographer, and former music industry attorney and artist manager, Sara Jane Boyers has returned to the world of children's publishing with a series of photo-illustrated book projects. Her focus remains on the arts with a bit of social activism thrown in, starting with her award-winning *Life Doesn't Frighten Me*, now celebrating twenty-five years in publication.

✳ ✳ ✳

The editor would like to thank the Estate of Jean-Michel Basquiat and all of the original collectors, art galleries, auction houses, and individuals who aided her in the research for the artist's images. That includes the late Gérard Basquiat; the historic Robert Miller Gallery; Galerie Bruno Bischofberger, Switzerland; and Galerie Enrico Navarra, Paris. Gagosian Gallery, New York, has been more than helpful in this anniversary edition update. Thanks are due as well to the office and estate of Dr. Maya Angelou and the Caged Bird Legacy Project, especially Colin Johnson, Rita Coburn Whack, and Mrs. Bettie Clay.

Illustration Credits

Front jacket, page 15: *Pez Dispenser* (1984), oil on canvas, 72 x 48". **Page 6:** *Masque* (n.d.), oil on canvas, 56 x 49½". **Page 9:** *Untitled* (1982), acrylic and oilstick on canvas, 68 x 60". **Pages 10—11:** *Boy & Dog in a Johnnypump* (1982), acrylic on canvas, 94.4 x 165". **Pages 12—13:** *Untitled* (1982), oil and acrylic on canvas, 70.8 x 150". **Page 14:** *Untitled* (1981), wax and crayon on paper, 12.2 x 17.3". **Pages 16—17:** *Self-Portrait* (1982), synthetic polymer paint and oilstick on linen, 76 x 94". **Page 19:** *World Crown Series* (1981), acrylic and spray paint on canvas, 56 x 47". **Pages 20—21:** *Untitled* (n.d.), acrylic and chalk on paper, 14 x 23". **Page 21:** *Untitled* (1984), acrylic and oilstick on canvas, 72 x 56¼". **Page 22—23:** *Profit 1* (1982), acrylic on canvas, 86.5 x 157.5". **Page 24:** *Snakeman* (1982/83), mixed media on paper, 22.4 x 30.1". **Page 26:** *Thirty-sixth Figure* (1983), acrylic on canvas, 60 x 47⅞". **Page 27:** *Formless* (1982/83), mixed media on paper, 22.4 x 30.1". **Page 28:** *Untitled* (1983), crayon on paper, 39.4 x 22.5". **Page 31:** *Ass Killer* (1984), acrylic and oil on canvas, 66.1 x 59.8". **Page 32:** © Dwight Carter. **Page 34:** © Lizzie Himmel.